SHARKY  GEORGE

SharkyandGeorge.com

OFFICIAL WARNING

THE RULES OF THIS BOOK ARE:

THERE ARE NO RULES!

TAKE OFF THE FRONT COVER, **FLIP IT OVER** AND **CREATE** YOUR OWN!

TAKE IT WHEREVER YOU GO . . .

foooosh
zoooomm

Zzzzzzzzzzzzzzzzzzzzzz

**THIS IS NOT A BOOK THAT MINDS GETTING A BIT ROUGHED UP.
DRAW** ON IT, **SPILL** ON IT, GET IT **MUDDY** . . . IT **WON'T CARE!**

This is the third 'W' in our book. Did you know that it is the only letter in the alphabet to have three syllables?

**AND REMEMBER . . .
NEVER RETURN TO A LIT FUSE.**

PLEASE SIGN HERE

Fill this page with as many signatures and autographs as you can
from famous people, friends and family, neighbours, anyone.
Make sure you get Sharky and George's too.

Postman

Mum/Dad

Famous person

SHARKY

Get Sharky to sign here

GEORGE

Get George to sign here

EGMONT

Sharky

George

KEY

(WHICH SYMBOL MEANS WHAT)

In the book you'll find these symbols to explain how to play the games, but just what do they all mean?

 **WHO?**

How many can play?

 **WHERE?**

Where's a good place to play the game?

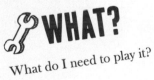 **WHAT?**

What do I need to play it?

HOW?

How do we get started? What are the rules?

First published in Great Britain 2013
by Egmont UK Limited
The Yellow Building, 1 Nicholas Road
London, W11 4AN
www.egmont.co.uk
Text copyright © Sharky and George Limited 2013
Illustrations copyright © Sebastien Braun 2013
The illustrator has asserted his moral rights.

ISBN 978 1 4052 5829 6
A CIP catalogue record for this book
is available from the British Library.
All rights reserved.

EGMONT
We bring stories to life

EGMONT LUCKY COIN

Our story began over a century ago, when seventeen-year-old Egmont Harald Petersen found a coin in the street.

He was on his way to buy a flyswatter, a small hand-operated printing machine that he then set up in his tiny apartment.

The coin brought him such good luck that today Egmont has offices in over 30 countries around the world. And that lucky coin is still kept at the company's head offices in Denmark.

www.shar

★ CONTENTS ★

orge.co.uk

VITAL INFORMATION

SHARE AND SHARE ALIKE. WE'VE FILLED IN OUR MOST IMPORTANT FACTS, BUT WE WANT TO KNOW ALL ABOUT YOU!

Write your answers here

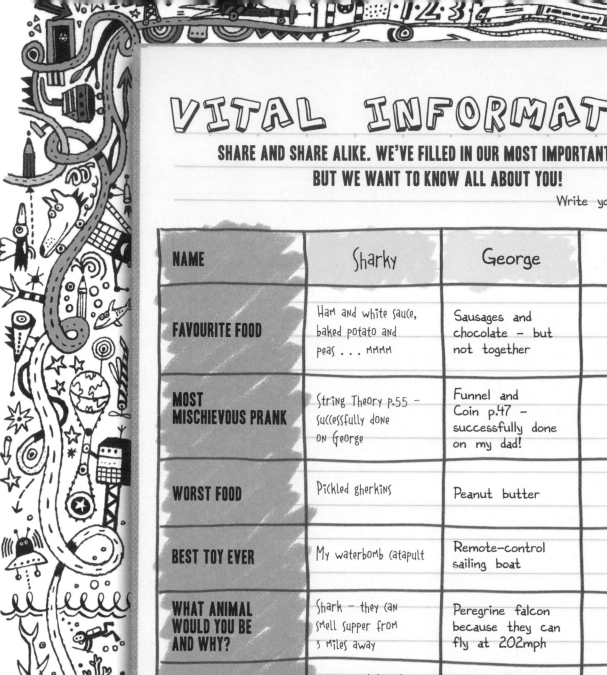

NAME	Sharky	George	
FAVOURITE FOOD	Ham and white sauce, baked potato and peas . . . MMMM	Sausages and chocolate – but not together	
MOST MISCHIEVOUS PRANK	String Theory p.55 – successfully done on George	Funnel and Coin p.47 – successfully done on my dad!	
WORST FOOD	Pickled gherkins	Peanut butter	
BEST TOY EVER	My waterbomb catapult	Remote-control sailing boat	
WHAT ANIMAL WOULD YOU BE AND WHY?	Shark – they can smell supper from 3 miles away	Peregrine falcon because they can fly at 202mph	
BEST ADVENTURE	When my dad took me sailing for the first time	Camping in the snow aged 10	
FAVOURITE GAME	Sandcastle Defence p.18	Bombers and Fighters p.8	
NICKNAME	Charlie Astor	Fluffy (it's the hair)	

NAME	Sharky	George	
FAVOURITE BOGEY TYPE	Big crusty ones that flick well	Long stringy ones	
WORST HABIT	Flicking bogeys! See above	Farting in the bath p.41	
THE SPORT YOU'RE BEST AT	Extreme boules p.38	Sailing	
IF YOU COULD BREAK A WORLD RECORD, WHAT WOULD IT BE?	I already did, for the fastest 100m as a pantomime horse!	The biggest ever game of Grandmothers' Footsteps	
FAVOURITE TYPE OF FART	Short but sweet	Loud and proud	
BEST MODE OF TRANSPORT	Space hopper	Sailing boat	
YOUR HERO	Mum	~~Willy Wonka~~ Sharky	
BEST RECIPE	Chocolate Biscuit Cake	Sticky Fried Goo Goo	
FAVOURITE BOOK (apart from this one)	Swallows and Amazons	Charlie and the Chocolate Factory	

KEEP YOUR EYES PEELED FOR . . .

PRANKS! Look out for the prank stamp in the book:

PRANKOMETER

Likely expression of your victim and escape measures . . .

 Victim is highly amused, no harm done – and you might even get a pat on the back.

 Still amused, nothing to worry about but your victim may look to get you back.

 Less amused this time, and already planning revenge.

 Not amused at all, get to a safe distance and watch your back.

 Don't wait around to find out, just run – run and hide.

⟹ REMEMBER! ⟸

Pranks are great – there is no doubt that they can be very funny but it is important to get it right. Choosing your victim is key to the whole process. The best pranks are played on your friends, or people who won't really mind and are most likely to laugh. Always remember that as soon as you do a prank on someone, they are allowed to get you back!

We would lean towards your dad for practical jokes, as mums prefer nice things like you making them breakfast in the morning – and your mum will be useful protection if your dad doesn't see the funny side . . .

Sharky   George

BOG FLUSH IT

 **10-50**

Imagine . . . you are a loo/ toilet/public convenience/ bathroom facility. No, really.

WHAT?

☆ Nothing – not even a bathroom.

☆ We reckon you need a Catcher for every 10 players. (1-10 players = 1 Catcher, 11-20 players = 2 Catchers, and so on.) The rest of the players are Flushers.

WHERE?

☆ Any space is ace!

☆ A clear area with a boundary that isn't too big because you want everyone quite close together.

HOW?

☆ Start in the playing area. The Catcher needs to tag the Flushers. When caught, the Flusher must squat down, much like sitting on the loo, and raise one arm out to the side to become a Bog!

☆ To be rescued, a Flusher who is free must whizz over to a Bog and use their arm to flush the toilet whilst shouting, 'FLUUUSSSH', before rushing off to live another day . . . or flush another loo.

BLEURGH!

TOILET TRAINING!

Use the Bogs that have been caught to duck behind and weave around if the Catcher is hot on your heels.

Make sure you go to the loo before playing!

FACT
- The average person spends three whole years of their life sitting on the toilet.
- King George II of Great Britain died falling off a toilet on 25th October 1760.

2

*FLICK BOOK FUN

Before television was invented people entertained themselves with flick books.*

We have started a little story about a running man in the bottom corner. Look at the drawings below to learn how to finish it. Then flick all the pages to see your story unfold.

HOW TO . . . CREATE A FLICK BOOK

1. Draw a stick man like this in the bottom corner.

2. Draw it again, but move the arms down a tiny bit.

3. Now draw it with the arms down a bit more.

4. This is how you make a flick book. Tiny movements of arms or legs in each picture.

5. Or try making small changes to the background – a bird flying or a sun moving across the sky.

6. Find the blank corner in the book and continue the story!

*We can't confirm that this is true but it would seem like the next best thing to X Factor™.

40:40

10 OR MORE

Imagine you are trying to break into a prison to rescue your friends without being spotted by the Guard.

WHAT?

☆ A woodland or park with lots of trees and bushes.

☆ A tree, bush or circle of jumpers for the base.

HOW?

☆ Choose a player to be the Guard. Everyone else is a Rescuer.

☆ Gather at the base. The Guard closes his eyes and gives the Rescuers 40 seconds to go and hide.

☆ After 40 seconds the Guard starts searching. If he spots a Rescuer, he must race back to the base shouting, '40:40 I SEE SHARKY', and touch the base before Sharky (or whoever he has spotted).

☆ If the Guard gets to the base first, the Rescuer becomes a Prisoner and must sit at the base.

☆ If a Rescuer reaches the base, he can shout, '40:40 SAVE ALL'; then all the Prisoners are free to go.

☆ If the Guard catches all the Rescuers then a new Guard is chosen, and the game starts again.

40
40

IF I WERE YOU . . .

Make sure the Guard doesn't FOXY GUARD* or stay too close to the base. He must go out and try to find the Rescuers away from the base, otherwise the game will get too boring.

* FOXY GUARDING is the act of hanging around the base, which gives no chance for the Rescuers to SAVE ALL. If the Guard is foxy guarding, Rescuers should just sit tight and wait for him to venture further out.

G.

MORE RESCUERS – THEY NEED TO HIDE

A RESCUER 'SAVING ALL'

THIS IS THE BASE

THE GUARD – REMEMBER, NO FOXY GUARDING!

GOOD HIDING PLACE

5

FISHY FISHY FISHY

A little bit like British Bulldogs but with fish, not dogs. Oh, you'll get the idea. Just keep reading.

Fishy, Fishy, Fishy, come swim in the sea . . .

 ## WHAT?

☆ A rectangular room or space about 5-10 metres wide. This will be the sea.

☆ You probably need a Shark for every 15 players. (1-15 players = 1 Shark, 16-30 players = 2 Sharks, etc.) The rest of the players are Fishies.

FISH AND TIPS

Remember, the Funky Seaweed CANNOT move their feet or catch the Fishies.

Sharky,
    Sharky,
        Sharky
            you can't
                catch
                    me!

HOW?

☆ First, choose some Sharks to do the catching.

☆ All the Fishies start on one side of the room and the Sharks chant, 'Fishy, Fishy, Fishy, come swim in the sea,' and the Fishies chant back, 'Sharky, Sharky, Sharky, you can't catch me.'

☆ The Fishies then have to get to the other side of the room without being tagged by the Sharks.

☆ If a Fishy is caught, he becomes Funky Seaweed, and he must stay exactly where he is, keeping his feet still and waving his arms until all the Fishies are caught. The Funky Seaweed can't catch anyone, they just get in the way and wave around, rooted to the spot like their aquatic cousins!

☆ The Fishies who are still in must duck, weave and bob through the Funky Seaweed, trying to avoid the Sharks. The last remaining Fishy is the winner.

SHARKY & GEORGE — OFFICIAL PRANK

Get a friend or parent to put both thumbs together on the edge of a table. Challenge them to balance a glass full of water on their thumbs. When they accept the challenge, balance a big glass of water on their thumbs and step away. Now they are stuck, as there is no way for them to move the glass without spilling the water. You have them hostage until you decide they can be set free!

7

BOMBERS AND FIGHTERS

 12 OR MORE

The team that drops the most bombs is the winner.

Run! Run! Run!

WHAT?

☆ Tails for half the players (strips of material work pretty well).

☆ 2 buckets for each team.

☆ Markers for the base boundaries (cones, jumpers or rope).

☆ 30 coloured bombs per team (bottle tops, balls, stones, Connect Four™ discs).

HOW?

EACh team has two buckets - A and B.

Try to drop bombs in the other team's bucket A

 ← FULL

EMPTY →

Refuel your bomb supply from your own team's bucket B

FIRST TEAM TO EMPTY THEIR BUCKET B INTO THE OTHER TEAM'S BUCKET A WINS!

8

THIS FIGHTER IS AFTER A TAIL

NOT THAT SORT OF TAIL!

DROP THE BOMB

A

thanks

B

BASE

CONES, JUMPERS OR ROPE

HOW?

☆ Split into teams. Have as many teams as you like but each team needs a minimum of 6 players.

☆ Each team has an empty bucket A in a base circled by markers, and a bucket B filled with bombs.

☆ Within each team there are equal numbers of Bombers and Fighters. Decide who is going to be who.

☆ The Bombers have a tail (strip of material) hanging out the back of their clothing and must drop one bomb at a time into the other team's bucket A.

☆ The Fighters chase the Bombers. If they successfully remove the tail from a Bomber, their bomb is surrendered in exchange for their tail. The Bomber has to return to their bucket B to pick up another bomb.

☆ Fighters are not allowed to chase in their own base, so when a Bomber gets into base, they can stop running and concentrate on getting the bomb into the bucket.

IF I WERE YOU . . .

Get a referee to make sure everyone is playing by the rules:

* Only one bomb at a time for the Bombers

* Bombers must always have a tail showing when on a bombing run

* Bombers must surrender their bomb if their tail is removed

COPS AND ROBBERS

 10-50

 ## WHAT?

☆ Make a prison, which can be as simple as 4 jumpers in a square: 4 metres by 4 metres (about 5 long steps). It needs to be large enough to give the Robbers a chance of rescuing their captured comrades (mates).

 ## WHERE?

☆ An area with boundaries so the game isn't too unlimited. The more people playing, the bigger the area should be.

 ## HOW?

☆ Divide half the players into Cops and half into Robbers.

☆ The Cops give the Robbers 30 seconds to run away and then follow them out on the hunt.

☆ If a Robber is tagged then he must slope off into prison and stay there until he is rescued.

☆ To rescue the Robbers in prison, another Robber must run into the prison and then everyone who has been caught is free to go.

☆ If the Cops catch all the Robbers they win the game.

You live in a world where robbers run free around the country. An eager but relatively incompetent (useless!) police force is trying to restore order. And failing!

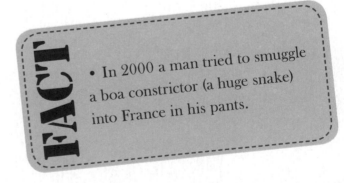

A BIT BELOW TO BENEFIT THE BOBBIES (COCKNEY FOR COPPERS . . . COPS!)

For this game it's best to work in teams. You may want to leave a few Cops to protect the prison, and then get the remaining Cops to hunt in pairs for the Robbers (so you can perform pincer movements and ambushes on lone Robbers). Work out a strategy that works best for you.

FACT

• In 2000 a man tried to smuggle a boa constrictor (a huge snake) into France in his pants.

GET ALL OF YOUR FRIENDS TO PUT A FINGERPRINT ON THIS PAGE. TO GET A

Sharky

George

FINGERPRINT, PRESS A FINGER ON AN INKPAD, OR IF YOU COLOUR YOUR FINGERTIP WITH A FELT TIP PEN AND THEN PRESS ON THE PAGE, THAT WORKS PRETTY WELL TOO. TRY THIS WITH MUD, CHOCOLATE, PAINT! HERE ARE SHARKY AND GEORGE'S THUMBPRINTS TO START YOU OFF.

FILL YOUR PANTS

or trousers or tracksuit bottoms

I am stuffed!

4 OR MORE

A scavenger hunt with a difference.

In other words, another silly Sharky and George version of a classic game!

HOW?

☆ Tuck your trousers into your socks.

☆ Make sure you are wearing baggy trousers.

☆ Run around the house collecting all of the items on the list.

☆ The very serious rule is that each item must go into your pants or trousers when you have found it!

☆ First one back with all the items is the winner, OR after 5 minutes each player must return to the kitchen where an umpire counts up who has the most items from the list.

☆ You can either use our list or make your own . . .

YOUR LIST . . .

....

....

....

....

....

SHARKY AND GEORGE'S LIST

* Toothpaste tube

* A post-it note

* An umbrella (Never open a brolly inside. We were told it is bad luck.)

* A cushion

* A balloon (a bonus point for the most inflated balloon)

* A book (a bonus point for the one with the most pages) (an extra bonus point if it's THIS book!)

* An egg (walk carefully!)

* A high-heeled shoe

* An ice cube (a bonus point for the biggest ice cube at the end of the game!)

COLLECTION CLUES
Collect ice cubes and eggs last, so they don't melt or break.

12

OFF THE GROUND IT

 **5 OR MORE**

 **WHAT?**

☆ A room with old tatty furniture, a playground, or if you have mats or even newspaper, you can play in an empty space or garden.

 **HOW?**

☆ Choose a Catcher for every 15 players. The rules are like *Tag* or *It*.

☆ However, in this game you are safe if you are NOT touching the ground.

☆ There is a problem though . . . if another player runs over and joins you on your piece of furniture/cushion/mat/chair/climbing frame (we could go on but we think you get the idea!), then whoever was there first has to move immediately and find another spot.

☆ We know it sounds unfair but in this game it is 'first come, second served'.

☆ If you are tagged you become the Catcher and the old Catcher is free to run away and stand on something.

Super-tag! With furniture! Not your parents' good furniture though!

HANDY HINTS TO STAY OUT OF TROUBLE . . .

Don't take refuge/stand on your mum's best sofa, your dad's newspaper if he hasn't read it yet, or your brother or sister's teddy bear/iPod/supper.

 ← Oops!

WIDE GAME

 10 - 40

This is an enormous game of **Stuck in the Mud** mixed with a bit of **Hide and Seek**. And it is **WIDE.**

 WHAT?

☆ Absolutely nothing, zilch, squat!

(That last one is not an order to crouch down immediately but another way of saying that you really don't need anything . . . So stand back up, this isn't Bog Flush It from page 2.)

 WHERE?

☆ An area of woodland or a large garden.

☆ Anywhere with a bit of space to run and lots of places to hide.

☆ Make sure you set the boundaries first so the area isn't too big.

 HOW?

☆ Divide into 2 equal teams: Catchers and Runners.

☆ The Catchers give the Runners one minute to hide.

☆ The Catchers must work together to catch everyone – if they spot a Runner and tag them, that person has to stand still.

☆ If a Runner is caught, he can be rescued by a member of his team (the Rescuer crawls through his legs).

☆ The Catchers win when they've caught all the Runners.

ENEMY AVOIDANCE ADVICE

CATCHERS' CLUES

Keep a careful eye on the Runners that you have caught!

Runners, stay low in your hiding places until you have to move. Use your stealth training to stay undetected (see page 60). Run and hide, people, run and hide.

ANIMAL GAME

○ Tell everyone that you are playing animal charades and choose 1 player to be the actor.

○ Take him outside and tell him to act like an animal (a cat, a monkey or an elephant for example) while everyone else guesses what he is.

○ Here is the mischievous bit! Make sure you have told another player which animal the actor is going to be. That player tells everyone else before the actor returns.

○ The rule is for everyone to guess every animal EXCEPT the correct one.

○ The actor will get really annoyed that everyone is being so stupid and unable to follow his brilliant acting! Keep him going as long as you can!

PRANK RATING

FACT
• Giraffes can clean inside their own ears with their 53 cm tongues.

Check no one is watching . . .
sure . . . now you try it!
If you can't touch your ear,
try your nose.

FACT
• Giraffes' vocal chords are so long that they often don't make any noise. So sadly they can't really show off to their mates about the whole tongue/ear thing.

"who am I?"

HIPPO HOT POTATO

 10-50

A bit like Piggy in the Middle and Hot Potato, but with more chance of getting splashed.

WHAT?

☆ About 20 water bombs already filled and knotted.

WHERE?

☆ Outside ONLY!

HOW?

☆ Everyone, apart from the chosen Hippo, makes a circle.

☆ The Hippo stands in the middle of the circle.

☆ A person in the circle takes a water bomb and throws it to someone else in the circle.

☆ You are not allowed to hold the water bomb for more than 1 second.

☆ The Hippo tries to smash the water bomb while it's in the air.

☆ If the Hippo succeeds then the thrower of the water bomb becomes the Hippo.

☆ If someone in the circle drops the water bomb, they become the Hippo.

HIPPO HINTS

If you're in the circle, try a dummy throw of the water bomb to put the Hippo off. You can also play this game with more than one water bomb at a time to make it a bit trickier. G.

FACT

• A really fat daddy hippo weighs up to 3,600kg, which is about the weight of 3 cars.

SANDCASTLE DEFENCE

 **2 OR MORE**

Pretend that you have built a wooden castle, and a sea of lava has been sent by an evil emperor to destroy it . . .

 **WHAT?**

☆ A tidal beach, preferably with the tide just starting to come in.

☆ Spades.

HOW?

FACT

• The tallest sandcastle ever made was 19 metres high on Fiesta Island in San Diego.

See if you can beat it . . . aim high!

☆ Split into 2 teams.

☆ Draw a back line in the sand about 30 big paces away from the sea. Don't build behind this line.

☆ You want to give yourself at least half an hour to build your sandcastle and defence before the sea starts 'attacking'!

☆ Each team builds a huge and well-defended sandcastle.

☆ Put a feather, flag or seaweed on the top, and whichever is the last thing to fall into the sea is the winning castle.

☆ If you just want to build one castle together that is fine; it doesn't have to be a competition.

How long will it last?

IF I WERE YOU:

Build as many sea defences as you can, and when things get really desperate, parents lying down in front of the castle make pretty good wave breakers!

Don't go near the sea without your parents. And be careful with little brothers and sisters!

Increase the stakes by getting a grown-up to sponsor the competition so that the winning team gets an ice cream (or if you're all getting one, the winners get a flake in theirs).

If you're on the losing team, try appealing to a grown-up's softer side and see if you can wangle an ice cream by saying: 'It's not the winning, it's the taking part that counts!'

MORPH

Build a new sand body for your dad: give him a mermaid tail or a mermaid top!

DRIBBLE CASTLES

 2 OR MORE

Jazz up your normal sandcastle with a dribble castle.

🔧 WHAT?

☆ Hands – 2 each.
☆ A bucket, maybe . . .

 HOW?

☆ Perch yourself on the sand, just about where the sea reaches the beach when a wave breaks.

☆ Take a big handful of really wet sand and let it dribble slowly out of the bottom of your hand on to a patch of dry sand nearby.

☆ You can also fill a bucket full of wet sand if you want to build further up the beach.

☆ Do this again, and again, and again, until you have the tallest tower that you can possibly make.

What a corker!

nearly there!

CONSTRUCTION CLUES

Don't worry if the skinny tower collapses at first. It will create a fantastic foundation for the rest of your dribble castle.

Ⓢ

FACT

DARE!

• A narrow strip of sand pointing from the beach out to sea is called a spit. Find one and see how far you can spit on a spit. If anyone tells you off say it is geography homework!

DEMOLITION

Building tall structures or towers is great. Smashing them down again is greater.

 **2 OR MORE**

WHAT?

☆ Lots of flat rocks and sand.

HOW?

☆ Build the highest tower possible by balancing flat rocks on top of each other (a tower of 5 or more is pretty good).

☆ Use sand as cement to wedge the rocks together and make the tower sturdy.

☆ Take it in turns to demolish the tower. Go and find a good handful of rocks to use as demolition 'bombs'.

Don't stand near the tower of stones — you don't want to get hit.

TOWER TOPPLING TIPS

Make sure your demolition bombs are not too big and heavy to throw accurately at the tower, but not too small and weedy to knock it over either. Save your best flat stones for stone skimming on page 25.

OLDER PEOPLE ARE BETTER AT THROWING SO MAKE THEM START FURTHER AWAY. Here is a handy table:

1 year old	Don't be silly, one year olds can barely crawl, let alone throw.
2 year old	Still optimistic, these guys need to master walking first.
3 year old	OK they can have a go from 3 paces away but we reckon they'll struggle.
4 year old	4 paces back.
5 year old	5 paces back.
6 year old	6 paces back.
7 year old	23 paces back . . . only joking, 7 paces back . . . I think you get the idea . . .

When building your tower aim to put the biggest, flattest rocks at the bottom and gradually balance smaller and smaller rocks on top.

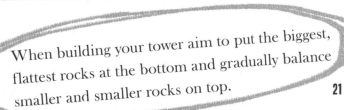

DAMS

Dams control river flow, store water and produce hydro-electricity. If you are at the right beach you can do this too . . . except for the making electricity bit . . . unless you have a cat with you (see page 83).

Here's one of my faves from my hydro-electric power station photo album. G.

A lot of beaches will have a little stream of water running into the sea. Best to go to the top of the beach and see if you can find the source. (Avoid a smelly stream as you might have found a sewage drain!)

If you find a nice clean, shallow stream choose a spot that isn't too wide and start building a wall of sand (a dam) across the middle.

When you have built your dam, you will need to keep making the wall higher so the water doesn't overflow. Make the wall nice and thick too so it doesn't collapse.

When you have got lots of water behind your dam, the fun bit is to break it! Collect big rocks to bomb the dam and destroy it.

HELP!

MY SAND KEEPS GETTING WASHED AWAY BECAUSE THE STREAM IS TOO FAST! WHAT TO DO?

OK, maybe it is a bit tricky, but if you are determined then carry on reading. You need to find some large rocks and build a wall all the way across the stream.

Fill in as many of the cracks as you can with smaller stones and pebbles. You can even get some seaweed or grass to fill the gaps.

Once that is done, shovel sand all over your foundations and that should do the trick.

FACT

• Have you ever dreamed that you can fly? Well, there is a big sea bird called an albatross that can fly while it is asleep. Impressive!

ZZZZZ

stop snoring!

23

DUNE BALL ROLLERCOASTER

 **1 OR MORE**

 **WHAT?**

☆ A ball (any size will do, although somewhere between a marble and tennis ball is perfect).

Make the most elaborate (that means fancy) and fantastic rollercoaster for a ball.

TOTALLY AMAZING!

 **HOW?**

☆ Find a reasonably steep slope (it could be a sand dune or one of those ramps that boats go down to get into the sea; make sure there aren't any boats using the ramp though).

☆ Draw out a rough rollercoaster pathway with a stick; make it like a snake, all twisty and curvy.

☆ Then, using handfuls of wet sand, start to build up the corners, and use the ball to shape the track that it will eventually be rolling down.

☆ You have to use a bit of trial and error here – try the ball out on each corner to see if it will roll down without help.

☆ The aim is to create a long rollercoaster track that the ball runs down on its own. You could also build tunnels and bridges for the ball to go through, and even jumps if you're feeling ambitious.

COMPETITIVE EDGE

If you'd like to compete with someone else, choose a start and finish line. Build a rollercoaster for the ball (the more corners, tunnels and jumps there are, the longer it will take the ball to reach the bottom). First one to the finish line is the winner.

STONE SKIMMING

Hold your stone like this

 **1 OR MORE**

🔧 **WHAT?**
⭐ Perfect flat stones or shells.

🌍 **WHERE?**
⭐ The sea, a river, pond, lake or moat!

How many times can you get a flat stone/shell to skip along the water?

 HOW?

⭐ Select a smooth, flat, round stone that fits between your thumb and your pointing finger.

⭐ Fit the stone neatly along the length of your thumb and pointing finger, so that about half of the outside edge of the stone is covered.

⭐ Then get close to the water, crouch down low, and throw the stone with a flick of your wrist almost level with the water.

⭐ The aim is to get the stone to bounce as many times as possible on the surface of the water.

FACT
• The WORLD RECORD for stone skimming is 51 skims!
Beat that!

HIGH SCORES

Your record is ☐

George's record is ☐ 10

Sharky's record is ☐ 14

Make sure you write it in pencil so you can always rub it out when you get a higher score.

PEBBLE POINTER
Stone selection is key. The flatter, smoother and rounder, the better.

Round flat stone: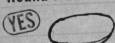
YES

Slate:
YES

Chicken:
NO

iPhone:
PERFECT BUT NO.

CRAB HUNTING

1. HANDLING CRABS

You may have noticed that crabs have some pretty serious nippers, and if you're going to catch them you don't want to get pinched. Pick one up between your thumb and pointing finger at the widest part of the shell, so their claws cannot reach your fingers . . . be brave!

> Here are some tips for catching the best and biggest crabs.

Shopping list:

* a long bit of strong string (at least 10 metres, or a proper crabbing line if you can get one)

* bacon (crabs' favourite food) tied to one end of the string

* a small weight or stone tied just below the bacon on the string

2. CATCHING CRABS IN ROCK POOLS

Look carefully around rock pools:
- in cracks, nooks and crannies
- under thick seaweed
- under thin layers of sand

3. CATCHING CRABS FROM A HARBOUR WALL OR PIER

Gently lower your line into the water until the weight and bacon are resting on the bottom. If you're lucky, a crab will grab on to the bacon. You need to CAREFULLY hoist him out of the water and into your bucket (which must have some seawater in it to keep the crabs alive). Once you have caught a few crabs you can race them!

If the crabs aren't biting then look for some local knowledge. Find someone who lives nearby, not a tourist, and see if they know where the best crabbing spots are.

YUM

CRAB RACING

 **1 OR MORE**

Going horse racing can be expensive. This is a cheaper version but no less exciting!

 **WHAT?**

☆ At least 2 crabs.

☆ A ramp or beach sloping down to the sea.

Don't always go for the biggest crabs; often the speedy little ones run the fastest.

(S)

 HOW?

☆ Take your bucket of crabs and gently tip it over at the top of the ramp or the beach. Everyone playing the game chooses the crab they reckon will win.

☆ The crabs instinctively know the direction to the sea, and they'll scuttle towards the water.

☆ The first crab to reach the sea wins the race.

RACING CRUSTACEANS (that's another big word for crabs or anything with a hard shell on the outside – like a lobster). And a smartie? No.

If in doubt, go for the one with that winning look in their eyes!

G.

ROCK POOL TOP TRUMPS

 **2 OR MORE**

Similar to normal Top Trumps, but you score points for whatever you catch. There are two different versions of the game.

 ## WHAT?

☆ A net each.

☆ A bucket each.

☆ Rock pools.

 ## HOW?

☆ To score points, use the list below.

☆ You can only score once for each type of thing you catch (so 15 shrimps only gets you 7 points).

① GET FISHING

Try to scoop as many different things out of the rock pools.

Collect them in your bucket, but make sure there is a bit of seawater at the bottom so that everything stays alive.

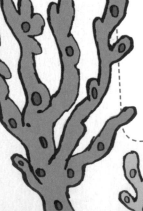

SEAWEED	2 points
SHELL (EMPTY)	3 points
SHELL (LIVING)	5 points
SHRIMP	7 points
PRAWN	8 points
CRAB	15 points
FISH	18 points
STARFISH	25 points
SEAHORSE	100 points

EYES, LEGS AND FINS

Same rules but different scoring system: this is all about eyes, legs and fins!

Everyone sets out with a net and bucket with seawater.

Once you have returned to base camp with your catch, the scoring begins.

1ST PLACE The person with the most eyes in their bucket.

2ND PLACE The person with the most legs in their bucket.

3RD PLACE The person with the most fins in their bucket.

Fishy **FACT**

• If you scoop your net under overhanging seaweed on the sides of rock pools, that's where shrimps, prawns and fish like to hang out.

If you find a very rare 10-legged, 17-eyed lobster-fish with a quiff in the shape of a fin you have basically won . . . .

G.

Have a look among the rock pools for some flat rocks or stones for the games on page 21 and page 25.

S

Check out the crab-hunting tips on page 26 to improve your score.

WAVE HURDLES

2 OR MORE

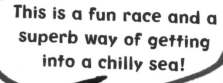

This is a fun race and a superb way of getting into a chilly sea!

WHAT?

☆ Some waves – but not too big!

HOW?

☆ Scratch a start line in the sand about 15 big footsteps away from where the waves come up the beach.

☆ Everyone lines up along the start line and the oldest person shouts: 'On your marks, get set, GO'.

☆ Then run as fast as you can towards the sea and jump over every single wave in your path. Count out loud as you jump over each one so you can tell who is winning!

☆ The person who gets furthest out to sea before falling over or hitting a wave is the winner.

WOOF

I win!

WATER KILLER BALL

 **4 OR MORE**

 ## WHAT?

☆ A spongy foam ball or a beach ball.

 ## WHERE?

☆ The sea (or a swimming pool).

Messing around at the beach in the shallows can be dangerous. You might get eaten by a shark, stung by a jellyfish, knocked over by a wave, taken out by a rip current or, worse still, get hit on the head by a squidgy ball.

HOW?

☆ A person is the Killer at the start and they are the only one allowed to touch the ball. If anyone is being sissy about the chilly sea then go back one page.

☆ The Killer closes their eyes and counts to 10 while everyone else in the water disperses (this means run/swim away!)

☆ The Killer chucks the ball at people, trying to hit them.

☆ If you get hit by the ball you become a Killer and must hit the other players with the ball. Wait until the ball is thrown to you to catch them out.

☆ The last free player is the winner, and is the Killer for the next round.

SAFETY STEPS

Duck underwater if the ball is coming towards you.

If ducks played this game would they have to 'human' underwater? Just a thought!

ULTIMATE BEACH FRISBEE

 8-30

Like netball or football but with a frisbee instead of a ball, and 'score zones' instead of a goal.

WHAT?

☆ A frisbee and two teams.

HOW?

☆ First, draw a rectangular pitch in the sand. It can be any size, depending on how many players there are and how far you want to run!

☆ For five-a-side you probably want it about 10 beach towels long and 6 beach towels wide.

☆ Draw big boxes at each end of the pitch to mark out the score zones (look at the drawing below).

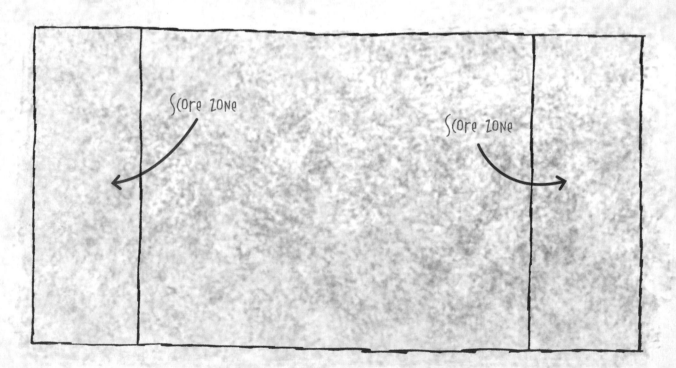

Score zone

Score zone

THE RULES ARE SIMPLE . . .

☆ Each team stands in their score zone. One player starts the game by throwing the frisbee to the other team.

☆ If you catch the frisbee you can't move your feet, so to get it up the pitch you have to throw it to another teammate.

☆ If the frisbee is dropped you must pass it to the other team.

☆ To score a point, you have to throw the frisbee to a member of your team, who must catch it in the opposition's score zone. Goooaaaal!

Try this!
CROCODILE CATCH METHOD

FACT
• Crocodiles have been around since dinosaurs were alive – 240 million years to be precise!

DEPENDS HOW NICE YOU ARE FEELING BUT . . .

For the younger ones, you can make a rule that they only have to touch the frisbee rather than catch it (but only if you are feeling generous).

You can make it more difficult by drawing smaller score zones.

TOWEL RACE

  **2 OR MORE**

 **WHAT?**

☆ 2 towels per team.

Imagine that you are faced with a river of lava. You can't touch it or you will burn your feet! (This might not be hard to imagine if the sun is out and heating up the sand!)

HOW?

☆ Mark out a course with a start and finish line. (A good place to start is next to your mum's purse and a good place to finish is by the ice cream van.)

☆ Split into teams of about 4 people.

☆ Each team stands on a towel behind the starting line and puts the second towel in front of them.

☆ Once you hear the word 'GO', hop on to the towel in front. Your feet cannot touch the sand. Then pass the first towel forward and put it down so everyone can hop on to that one. And so on until you cross the finish line and to glory! (And ice creams!)

RIDDLE: What gets wetter as it dries?
The clue is in the title!

DIG A HOLE

Some holes we have dug . . . .

The "Bunker"

The "Double-Dipper"

The "Tunnel"

Wonderful stuff!

THREE-STICKS

> **A more fun version of Long Jump.**

 **2 OR MORE**

WHAT?

☆ It's all in the name . . . Three Sticks, each about a metre long.

HANDY HINTS

☆ Make sure you have a really good run up when the gaps get bigger.

☆ Be extra careful on the first round so that you don't get knocked out at the start.

☆ Grown-ups are good at this game as they have longer legs, obviously, so if you make the gaps small enough you should be able to knock them out in the first round! No one likes a smug grown-up!

① ② ③

HOW?

☆ Lay the sticks next to each other in the sand, about a foot-width apart.

☆ Take it in turns to put ONE foot between sticks 1 and 2, the next foot between sticks 2 and 3, making sure the sticks do not shift AT ALL.

☆ Once everyone has had a go, spread the sticks a bit further apart.

☆ In each round, make the gaps between the sticks bigger, until you have to take a massive leap from gap to gap.

☆ It's meant to be a knock-out competition, but give everyone a good warm-up round to start.

FACT

• A kangaroo can jump 3 metres high and 8 metres in length.

• A flea can jump 200 times its own body length. That is the same as your mum or dad jumping over 7 football pitches.

These are all good reasons not to play Three-Sticks with a kangaroo, a really big flea . . . or your parents!

SEAWEED TAILS

 **4 OR MORE**

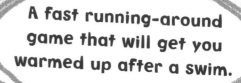
A fast running-around game that will get you warmed up after a swim.

 WHAT?

☆ A bit of seaweed each.

HOW?

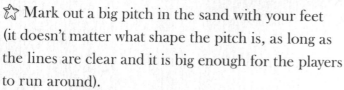

☆ Mark out a big pitch in the sand with your feet (it doesn't matter what shape the pitch is, as long as the lines are clear and it is big enough for the players to run around).

☆ Each player sticks a long bit of seaweed down the back of their swimmers, so that they have a long seaweed tail.

☆ When you hear the word 'GO', run around inside the pitch trying to pull out other people's tails.

☆ If your tail is pulled out, you become a Starfish and stand exactly where you lost your tail, wiggling your arms to get in the way of anyone else who is still playing the game. It's really important that the Starfish keep their feet stuck to the ground.

☆ The last person left with a seaweed tail is the winner.

SEAWEED WIGS

Once you've had enough of running with seaweed in your pants, try a seaweed wig-off.

Have a competition to see who can make themselves the best seaweed wig.
There are loads of different coloured seaweeds, so get imaginative, and the bigger the hairdo the better!

G.

TIP AND RUN

Cricket, without all the boring bits and the soggy jam sandwiches.

 **3-20**

WHAT?

⭐ A cricket bat or the nearest thing you can find to a bat.

⭐ A tennis ball.

⭐ Stumps (a tree, picnic box, stick in the ground or an upright boogie board).

⭐ A marker about 15 paces (or 7 really big jumps) away from the stumps.

SUBSTITUTE CRICKET BATS THAT WORK:
* tennis racket
* rounders bat
* a fat stick Ⓢ

SUBSTITUTE CRICKET BATS THAT DON'T WORK:
* large surf board
* medium-sized fish
* large '99' ice creams (unless they have a huge flake) G.

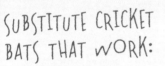

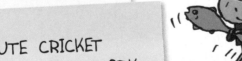

HOW?

⭐ Choose a Batsman and a Bowler; everyone else is a Fielder.

⭐ The Batsman stands in front of the stumps, and the Bowler throws the tennis ball towards the stumps.

⭐ The Batsman tries to stop the ball from hitting the stumps by whacking it.

⭐ If the bat makes contact with the ball in any way, shape or form, the Batsman HAS TO run out to the marker and back.

⭐ The Fielders must get the ball back to the Bowler as soon as possible so he can throw it towards the stumps.

⭐ If the Batsman gets back to the stumps before the Bowler throws the ball, he makes one run. If the Bowler hits the stumps, the Batsman is out.

⭐ Just as in cricket, the Batsman is out if the ball is caught without bouncing. Take it in turns to be Batsman and Bowler until everyone has had a go.

I normally play one hand, one bounce. It's just easier!

TOP TIPS

Don't worry about bowling the ball like in cricket, a good under-arm throw should do the trick. A boogie board sticking out of the sand makes a very handy wicket, as long as you support it with lots of sand.

EXTREME BOULES

 2 OR MORE

An extreme sport is one where there is an element of danger and adventure. You need to be brave, tough and willing to go beyond the limits of normal people. Unfortunately Extreme Boules is nothing like this. But it is a really fun way to make normal boules more exciting . . . !

WHAT?

☆ 2 boules each. Boules can be tennis balls, cricket balls or shoes. Not normal boules!

☆ A jack. (This is the thing you aim for with your boules.)

 If you have a friend (called Jack, use him.

If Jack wants to play and doesn't want balls thrown in his general direction, then you can use any of the following: a golf ball, shell, mini windmill . . . anything smaller than the boule!

G.

HOW?

☆ The youngest person draws a throw line, and chucks the jack anywhere they like (the more imaginative the better – uphill, downhill, behind a rock, round a corner, on top of a sandcastle . . . though do not interrupt a game of Sandcastle Defence, see page 18).

☆ Each person takes it in turn to throw a boule towards the jack.

☆ Then everyone takes it in turns to throw the second boule.

☆ The boule that finishes closest to the jack wins, and that person gets a point.

☆ The winner also becomes the person to choose the throw line and chuck the jack for the next round.

HELPFUL HINDRANCES

When you are chucking the jack, aim to make it as tricky as possible for everyone. If you can, introduce extra rules like, 'for this round, you have to throw your boule between your legs' or, 'for this round, your throws only count if your boule bounces off that rock'.

TOXIC

BUTT DARTS...

A serious accuracy challenge, and good practice for those moments when you really need the loo in the car and you just have to hold on.

 **2 OR MORE**

 **WHAT?**

☆ A 10p coin.

☆ A large mug.

 **HOW?**

☆ Place the mug on the ground, and choose a start line about 5 big steps away from it.

☆ Take it in turns. The first player clenches the coin between their butt cheeks and carefully waddles towards the mug. Take careful aim over the mug and release. Gently!

☆ If you miss, you're knocked out. If you manage to do it, usc 2 coins for round two, 3 coins for round three and so on! The winner is the last person left.

HA HA HA!

It's easier if you're wearing baggy trousers.

CLENCHING CLUES

Adopt the penguin waddle with your feet together. Try to avoid farting on the approach as you arc sure to lose your grip! Mainly because you should be chuckling heartily at this point.

(AND FARTS)

Keep a log of your farts throughout a whole day with this handy table, to find out if you are above or below average. ⑤

GUFF-O-GRAPH

Tick the correct box on the Guff-o-Graph each time you let rip.

Short and to the point	
Long and Squeaky	
Loud and proud	
Silent but violent	

WHILE WE ARE ON THE SUBJECT

FART FACT 1
The average human farts 16 times a day.

FART FACT 2
In ancient Japan, public contests were held to see who could fart the longest and loudest.

FART FACT 3
If you fart non-stop for 6 years and 9 months, enough gas is produced to create the energy of an atomic bomb!

THE BATHTIME TECHNIQUE

If you are a hoarder and want to build a collection of farts, then read on . . .

Step 1: Eat baked beans for supper.

Step 2: Hop in the bath with a jam jar.

Step 3: Remove the lid and fill the jar with water.

Step 4: Keep the jam jar upside down underwater and let rip. As the bubbles rise you need to trap them in the jar. Catch as many as you can manage.

Step 5: Replace the lid on the jar while it is still underwater and upside down. Hey presto! Freshly caught farts.

Step 6: Go to a dark room, ask a grown-up to light a match and hold it really close to the lid. Open the lid and marvel at your ballistic bum!

MYSTERY MOULDY MODELLING

 **4 OR MORE**

Most of us can draw but can you shape and model your way to victory?

 **HOW?**

☆ Get a grown-up to write down lots of objects on pieces of paper, scrunch them up and put them into a pot. Or a hat.

☆ The first player picks a piece of paper and has 60 seconds to create the object with modelling clay.

☆ Whoever guesses it is the next sculptor. If no one guesses, the sculptor stays the same.

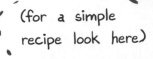 **WHAT?**

☆ Modelling clay.

☆ A timer or stopwatch.

☆ Paper and pen.

☆ Pot or hat.

(for a simple recipe look here)

Good examples are fork, sunglasses, boat, beans on toast.

Or a dog poo, challenger tank, happiness, a squirrel, a bum.

HUMAN SCULPTURE

Choose a person to be the sculptor. Everyone else stands together in the middle of the room. The sculptor moves people around and puts them into any position. If any of the players smile or giggle, they are immediately out of the game and have to make the other players laugh without touching them. The last person standing still 'in position' is the winner.

SCULPTING SUGGESTIONS

* A person picking another person's nose
* A boy holding hands with all the girls
* A person sitting on another person's back as if they're having a donkey ride
* Monkey poses

MODELLING CLAY RECIPE

WHAT?

⭐ 2 cups of plain flour

⭐ 1 cup of salt

⭐ 2 tablespoons of cream of tartar

⭐ 2 tablespoons of oil

⭐ 2 cups of water

⭐ 1 teaspoon of colouring

This is NOT for eating, but is the best way to make lots and lots of brilliant sculpting dough in any colour you like.

HOW?

⭐ Mix all the ingredients in a saucepan. Ask an adult to stir the mixture over a low heat until it goes lumpy. Keep stirring and it will soon go smooth and form a dough.

⭐ Remember to let it cool before playing!

⭐ Keep in an airtight container when you are not using it so it doesn't dry out.

Send a photo of your great sculptures to sharkyandgeorge.com.

CHICKEN FEED

2 TO 4 + 1 UMPIRE

A card game to test your speed and quick thinking . . . and ability to imitate a chicken (imitate means copy!).

WHAT?

☆ 2 packs of cards.

☆ A square or rectangular table.

HOW?

☆ Each Chicken (or player, but we prefer Chicken) stands on one side of the table.

☆ Scatter one pack of cards face up on a table so that they are not touching each other.

☆ Choose an Umpire (don't worry, the Umpire changes each round). The Umpire holds the other pack and slowly turns a card over.

☆ The Chickens have to find the same card on the table and drag it off their side of the table using just one finger. If you are caught using more than one finger, you have to sit out the next round!

☆ More than one Chicken can have their finger on the same card.

☆ The winner of each round gets 10 points BUT minus a point for every incorrect card knocked off the table on their side, so take extra care!

Chickens can't swallow while they are upside down.

PECKING POINTERS

Do not play with real chickens . . . you won't stand a chance!

Buy yourself some time by throwing a dummy. You do this by putting your finger on a random card so everyone will think you have found it first. While they are distracted you can be looking for the real one! Sneaky, eh?

Make sure you choose a table that is big enough to spread out all the cards but small enough so that everyone can reach the far side.

FACT

• The longest recorded flight of a chicken is 13 seconds.

CARD TRICK

Your friend picks any card from a regular deck and puts it on the top of the pack. You pick up the deck, shuffle it a bit, and find their card every time. How?

WHAT?

☆ This easy card trick is based on the 'key-card' principle in magic. By knowing the identity of just one card, you can find a selected card every time.

The King of hearts is the only character in a pack of cards with a moustache . . . interestingly!

HOW?

☆ Shuffle a pack of cards.

☆ Take a peek at the bottom card and remember it. This will be your key-card.

☆ Let your friend choose a card. Tell them to look at it and remember what it is, and then put it face down on the top of the deck.

☆ Ask your friend to divide the deck into halves and place the bottom half containing the key-card on top of the pile containing the chosen card. This is called 'cutting' the pack. Your key-card will now be resting on top of your friend's card.

☆ Let them cut the pack several more times as this will not mess up the order, but makes the trick look harder.

☆ Now turn the deck face up and look for the key-card. Your friend's card will be the one above it.

BEDROOM MINEFIELD

 1 OR MORE

Travel across your room without touching the ground!

  WHAT & WHERE?

☆ A MESSY BEDROOM!

Finally – an excuse not to tidy your room!

HOW?

☆ Start on your bed and use anything you can to move from the bed to the door. Books, pants or pillows are all your friends in this game as they provide stepping stones.

☆ If the bed is next to the door and you need a bit of a challenge, then maybe start by standing next to the window.

☆ The tidier the room, the more difficult the game!

☆ If you touch the floor you will set off a bomb, get eaten by crocodiles or get bitten by snakes . . . either way, something pretty uncomfortable!

If you have a really tidy room, chuck an old pack of cards into the air and use the cards as stepping stones.

MINEFIELD MISSION MASTERCLASS
DO use books, underpants, skateboards.
DO NOT use lego pieces, marbles, the cat.

FUNNEL AND COIN

OFFICIAL PRANK
SHARKY & GEORGE

 **WHAT?**

☆ A funnel.

☆ A coin.

☆ A glass of water.

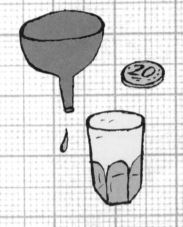

HOW?

☆ Put the thin end of the funnel down your trousers so the big open bit sticks out at your waist. Balance the coin on your forehead.

☆ Try to get the coin to drop into the funnel.

☆ Attempt it a few times and then ask your dad/ uncle/big brother to see if they can do it.

☆ Once they put the funnel in their trousers and the coin on their forehead, pick up a large glass of water that you have cunningly hidden nearby and pour the whole glass down the funnel!

PRANK RATING

ⓐ

et voilà!

ⓑ

← H_2O

ⓒ

THE CUSHION GAME

6 OR MORE

where am I going?

WHAT?

☆ A blindfold.

☆ A cushion.

But not a blindfolded cushion!

A blindfolded guessing-game where you sit on someone's knees and work out who they are by getting them to make a noise.

This one is a bit long-winded but stick with it as it is very funny to play!

G.

HOW?

☆ Clear a room and arrange chairs in a rough circle.

☆ Everyone sits down on the chairs.

☆ One person is blindfolded in the middle and spun round a few times. In the meantime, everyone changes seats as much as they want.

☆ The blindfolded person is handed a cushion. They must use this, not their hands, to feel their way to the circle of chairs. They have to find someone's lap, put the cushion on that lap and sit down.

☆ It is vital (really important) that everyone stays totally silent so that the blindfolded person can't work out who is sitting where.

☆ Once the blindfolded person is seated, they ask the person to make an animal noise. But get creative! You could say: 'make the noise of a mouse eating cheese' or, 'make the noise of a pig doing a fart'.

☆ The blindfolded person has to guess who the person is.

☆ If they get it right, the person making the noise becomes the blindfolded one.

☆ If they get it wrong, everyone has to hiss loudly, and the blindfolded person must look for a new lap to sit on. All the other players swap places again at this stage.

☆ If the blindfolded person is about to walk into a wall, or about to rest their cushion on a curled-up dog, the other players should hiss as a warning.

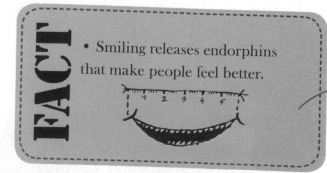

FACT

• Smiling releases endorphins that make people feel better.

So even if you find one of Sharky's jokes really unfunny, have a smile anyway. It will make him feel better too so everyone's a winner!

SHARKY & GEORGE OFFICIAL PRANK

PRANK RATING

SNEAKY SUGGESTION

If there is someone who thinks that they're really good at the game, get everyone to walk out of the room quietly when they are blindfolded! Watch through the door as they are busily trying to rest their cushion on empty chairs!

No giggling or you'll give the game away . . .

FACT
• Children laugh around 400 times a day but adults only laugh 15 times a day.

It must be very boring being grown-up so do your best not to become a grown-up!

Fancy a laugh?
OK here goes . . .

Why did the loo roll run down the hill?

To get to the bottom.

moo!

FRUITY PANTS

 **2 OR MORE**

Have you got **BIG PANTS?**
If so, then this is the game for you . . .

 ## WHAT?

☆ About 20 pieces of fruit or veg.

☆ 2 blindfolds.

HOW?

☆ Choose 2 people to be Hunters, blindfold them, and tell them to get on their hands and knees.

☆ Lay out all the fruit and veg on the floor in front of the Hunters. Then shout, 'GO!'

☆ The Hunters have 60 seconds to crawl around, gathering as many pieces as possible and stashing them down their pants!

☆ The important rule is that you have to carry every piece for it to be counted at the end, so it is worth wearing particularly large pants for extra storage.

Whenever you have a bit of fruit, if it has a sticker on it, then stick it here!

G. You can normally find them on apples and bananas.

PRANK RATING

Take your dad's newspaper and graffiti every photo. Here is a picture to practise on. Add a pimple, a beard and/or moustache, maybe a nice hat, some silly glasses and definitely some bogeys!

MURDER MYSTERY

 4 OR MORE

WHAT?

- ☆ A murderous imagination!
- ☆ 3 hats or bowls.
- ☆ Pen and paper.

> Beware of bizarre objects in strange places, and stay on your guard!

HOW?

☆ Each person is given a pen and 3 pieces of paper.

☆ On the first piece you write your own name.

☆ On the second you write a location anywhere in the house or garden.

☆ On the third you write a murder weapon. This can be anything from a toothbrush to a newspaper (but it has to be portable and in the house already).

☆ All the names go into one hat, the locations in another and the weapons in the last one. Give the hats a shake. Each player chooses a piece of paper from each hat.

☆ If you pick out your own name, put it back and choose another name – you can't kill yourself!

☆ You now have a victim, a location and a weapon.

☆ To kill your victim, you must hand them the weapon in the location. If your victim accepts the weapon then they are dead! They hand over their 3 pieces of paper and you have to murder their victim too.

☆ The winner is the person left alive at the end of the game!

When attempting to murder someone, they might well be expecting it, so it is a good idea to take them by surprise – just shove the weapon towards them and hope they grab it before they realise.

TIPS ON TOPPING YOUR VICTIM

It is a good idea to give boundaries so the locations aren't impossible.

G.

If you are at home and have a garden, you could do your murdering within the fence or wall of the garden.

SARDINES

3 OR MORE

Have you ever eaten sardines? They aren't very nice but they do come packed tightly in a nice tin. Being packed tightly in a small space is what this game is all about. Not fish.

WHAT?

☆ Sneakiness and cunning.

☆ The more players you have the more space and hiding places you will need.

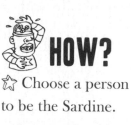

HOW?

☆ Choose a person to be the Sardine.

☆ The Sardine has to go and find a great hiding place. The spot must be big enough for all the players to hide there too. While the Sardine is looking for the hiding spot, everyone else closes their eyes and counts up to 60.

☆ When the players get to 60, everyone has to spread out and find the Sardine.

☆ If you find the Sardine, you become a Sardine and must hide with them. Be really quiet because you don't want to give away your position to other players.

☆ The last person to find the 'Tin of Sardines' is the loser . . .

On the plus side though, he gets to be the Sardine in the next round!

If you spot the Sardine, make sure no one else is around. Once the coast is clear, sneak in and hide, and try not to give the game away.

G.

52

SENIDRAS
(Sardines, but the other way round!)

How on earth do I play it backwards?

 3 OR MORE

HOW?

☆ This time round everyone except one person has to hide (the Searcher).

☆ The Searcher closes his eyes and counts backwards from 60 down to 0 (you see, I told you it was backwards).

☆ During the countdown, everyone else has to run and hide. It is **IMPORTANT** not to let the other players see where you hide, because if the Searcher finds someone they become a Searcher too (and they will know where you are).

☆ The last person to remain hidden is the winner.

• 1 million seconds is 11 days • 1 billion seconds is 31 years • 1 trillion seconds is 31,688 years •

If you want to count to 1 billion you better get going now!

Ⓢ

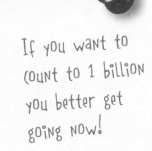

-but where are they all?

that's a lot of work!

53

PHOTO-TRICK-OGRAPHY

Taking endless photos of churches, your granny or the family can get a bit boring! Here are a few quick shots to make it a bit more interesting . . . and confuse your friends!

Send your photos to sharkyandgeorge.com!

click

TRY TO DO BETTER SHOTS THAN THESE, OR MAKE UP YOUR OWN SILLY ONES.

STRING THEORY

PRANK RATING

SHARKY & GEORGE OFFICIAL PRANK

WHAT?

☆ A ball of string.

HOW?

☆ Get a ball of string and make sure you have 2 different victims in your house, preferably mum and dad. They have to be in separate rooms for this to work.

☆ Take one end of the string to the first victim and ask if they wouldn't mind helping with an experiment; you can even say it is science homework. Your mum and dad will be very impressed that you are 'working' so hard, and they should be happy to help!

☆ Ask your first victim to hold the end of the string, then disappear around the corner and unravel the ball of string until you find your second victim. Cut the string and hand it to the victim. Ask them to hold the string while you go and get your 'measuring equipment'.

☆ You can then disappear and wait to see who is the first to realise they have been tricked into holding the end of a piece of string for no other reason than to give you a good giggle!

THE EGG CUP GAME

 **4 OR MORE**

> You need to be calm under pressure and to enjoy soaking your friends. No eggs were harmed in the making of this game.

WHAT?

☆ Pens.

☆ A jug of water.

☆ Paper.

☆ Be prepared to get wet!

☆ An egg cup.

HOW?

☆ Get everyone to sit in a circle on the floor or around a table.

☆ Choose a person to start the game (the Games Master).

☆ The Games Master selects a category and tells everyone what it is.

☆ Then everyone, including the Games Master, chooses one thing from that category, writes it on a piece of paper and puts it in their pocket until the end of the round.

☆ Categories could be: SPORTS, CHOCOLATE BARS, CARS, COUNTRIES (your geography teacher will be impressed!), COLOURS, etc.

☆ The Games Master fills an egg cup with water and walks around the circle, hovering the cup over each player's head while they shout out their own selection from the category.

☆ As soon as a player picks the Games Master's choice the water is tipped on their head.

☆ The Games Master must show his bit of paper to all the players as proof. If the wrong person got a soaking then they can pour an egg cup of water over the Games Master!

IF I WERE YOU . . .

For a fast-paced game, choose a category with not too many options . . . there aren't many types of big cat for example, which means you shouldn't have to wait long before your friends get a soaking.

You can use a mug, water bomb, egg or bucket of baked beans to raise the stakes!

G.

You might want to play these versions outside to avoid a telling-off.

S

BOOK MISSION

Sharky and George are right when they say NEVER follow your book on a mission.

WHAT?

☆ A book.

HOW?

Send this book on a mission.
WARNING: NEVER follow your book on a mission and DO NOT lean out of windows or over banisters.
Good luck, soldier!

ZIP WIRE IT

☆ Tie a piece of string or fishing line to a top floor window or high structure, and then tie the other end to something at ground level. Make sure the wire is really tight so the book can slide easily, and the angle is steep enough so the book can slide all the way down.

☆ Then put the book over a coat hanger and send it down the wire while humming the theme tune to Mission Impossible or James Bond.

wwOOOO.

PARACHUTE IT

☆ Open the book to the middle and tie some string around the spine.

☆ Then tie the string to the handle of an umbrella, take it to a top floor window and throw the umbrella out.

☆ Watch the book float slowly down . . .

RACE IT

☆ Attach your book to a roller skate, skateboard, toy car or other small-wheeled vehicle.

☆ Push it down a hill, and race it to the bottom on your bike. Or race your mates' books . . . whose is fastest?

BUNGEE JUMP IT

☆ Keep the string around the spine of the book from the parachute mission.

☆ Collect as many elastic bands as possible. The postman is always a good person to ask. Link the bands together as shown below to make your bungee cord.

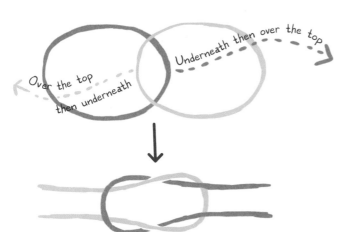

Over the top then underneath

Underneath then over the top

☆ Go to a stairwell and attach the end of your bungee cord with string to the railing. The book will be nervous so give it a moment to ready itself, then tip it over the edge and watch it bounce up and down. Adrenaline junkie!

59

SNIPER SEARCH

 4-20

You are a sniper who has to remain concealed from your enemy.

How long should I stay?

Don't move, it's so comfy!

sniff sniff

 ## WHERE?

☆ A large outside space (a garden, park or woodland), with lots of trees, bushes and long grass.

You can camouflage the Sniper(s) by covering them in grass, mud, and branches. Elastic bands are great to keep the camouflage in place around their arms and legs.

G.

 ## HOW?

☆ Split into 2 teams and pick a team name: for example, Alpha, Bravo, Charlie, Delta, Echo, Foxtrot, ~~Golf~~ George

☆ Select a member of each team to be the Sniper. If you have a large group you can choose 2 or 3 Snipers.

☆ Both teams choose a secret area to be their 'stealth zone' where they must camouflage their Sniper(s). Make sure the other team can't see your stealth zone so there is no spying.

☆ Both teams start at a central base between the stealth zones. On the word 'GO', teams race to their stealth zones and hide their Snipers.

☆ Once both teams are happy with their camouflage, leave the Sniper(s) in the stealth zone, run back to the central base and shout that you are ready.

☆ As soon as both teams are back at the base, the Sniper search begins.

☆ The first team to find the enemy's hidden Sniper(s) wins the game.

SNEAKY SUGGESTIONS

If you are feeling really sneaky you can make a decoy Sniper.

Do this by making a pile of leaves in the shape of a Sniper; you could even borrow the actual Sniper's shoes and have them sticking out the end!

This should waste the other team's time and give you a chance to find the enemy's Sniper(s) first.

Remember to make the plants covering your Sniper look natural; you never see the roots of grass or upside down bracken leaves in the wild.

If there is any bare skin showing on your Sniper(s), especially on the face, use wet mud as camouflage cream.

FACT

• The longest shot to hit its target by a sniper is 2,475 metres. That is the equivalent of from where you are to a very long way away!

Try to be first back to central base, otherwise the other team might see you hiding your Sniper(s).

STEALTH

 2-20

> You are a Secret Agent and your mission is to sneak up as close as possible to the enemy base without alerting the Guard.

WHAT?

☆ Completely camouflaged Secret Agents (using elastic bands and lots of grass, bracken, leaves, sand and wet mud).

WHERE?

☆ For this game you need dense woodland or very long grass, so there is plenty of cover. A big set of sand dunes or heather works well too.

 # HOW?

☆ Choose a person to be the Guard and the rest of the players are Secret Agents.

☆ The Secret Agents must all start from the same base.

☆ The Guard must run about 100 metres away from the Secret Agents, and then shout 'GO'. The Secret Agents have to get as close to the Guard as possible without being spotted, so the best ones must choose a route where they remain hidden from the Guard's gaze at all times.

☆ If the Guard sees a Secret Agent, he has to shout, 'I see you, Pippa' (or whatever their name might be). Pippa is now caught and must sit behind the Guard.

☆ The Secret Agent who gets the closest to the Guard without being spotted wins the game.

THE GUARD

SECRET AGENT

WATCH OUT !

STEALTH TIPS

You can make it harder for the Guard by saying he has to sit cross-legged on the ground, and spot the Secret Agents without any height advantage.

Ⓢ

FACT

• Girls can see better out of the corners of their eyes than boys. Seeing out of the corner of your eye is called peripheral vision.

Hmmm, not sure about that!

LASER RUN TIME TRIAL

AS MANY PLAYERS AS YOU CAN GET!

> You have been captured by the enemy and taken prisoner. You have to escape through a network of laser alarms without triggering them and alerting the enemy's attention.

WHAT?

☆ A path with trees, bushes or fencing on either side.

☆ Some colourful string, preferably red.

☆ A stopwatch.

HOW?

☆ Pick a player to be the Prisoner.

☆ All other players should work together to weave about 10 metres of string from one side of the path to the other.

☆ When weaving it along the path make sure you go low and high with the string, so the Prisoner can't just crawl along the ground or hop over the lines.

☆ Once you have a course, the Prisoner must try to make it through in the fastest time possible without touching the string. Every time the Prisoner touches the 'laser' you add a second to their time.

☆ Take it in turns to be the Prisoner. Use the stopwatch to time everyone and the person who is quickest, and has the least penalties, wins.

EASY

WHAT YOU DON'T WANT TO DO IS . . .

Put the lines too close together as it will be too difficult. Also, if they are too far apart then the course will be too easy. Just experiment until you have it about right.

BLINDFOLDED OBSTACLE COURSE

 2-20

You are trying to escape from an enemy prison at night. It is pitch black so you can't see a thing. You have to feel your way out as quickly as possible before the guards wake up.

WHAT?

⭐ A big ball of string.

⭐ And a short bit of string for each player.

⭐ A blindfold.

⭐ A stopwatch.

Am I close?

YES!

HOW?

⭐ Choose someone to set the string course.

⭐ This person should tie one end of the ball of string to a tree as the starting point. Then the mischief can begin!

⭐ Take the string under tree branches (so the Escapees will have to duck down and bump their heads – hee hee!); through thin gaps in trees (so they will get stuck between them if they've eaten too much for breakfast); and through puddles (so they will get their feet wet).

⭐ The string course can be as hard or as easy to follow as you like BUT do make it possible!

⭐ Each Escapee takes their short bit of string and ties a loop around the string at the start of the course. They are then blindfolded, and they set off along the course, one at a time, holding on to the looped bit of string. They mustn't let go until they have reached the end.

⭐ The quickest Escapee will earn his freedom!

AN ADVANCE WARNING!
Be careful some cheeky young scamp hasn't put the end of the line into a swamp!

DRAW A SCENE

We ran out of ideas for this page so we thought you could do a better job. Maybe draw a battle scene, your perfect house, garden or village. Plan an amazing new invention or map out a game you have made up.

ENEMY SPOTLIGHT

 2-20

You are an elite force attempting to storm the enemy base using the dark of night as cover.

WHAT?

☆ Night time.
☆ A powerful torch.
☆ A tree, bush or circle of jumpers as the prison.

WHERE?

☆ In the garden.

IF I WERE YOU . . .

HOW?

☆ Pick a player to be the Guard – they should be the only one with a torch. Everyone else is a Rescuer.

☆ Gather at an area you have chosen to be the enemy's prison. The Guard stands there too, then closes his eyes and gives all the Rescuers 40 seconds to run and hide.

☆ If the Guard sees anyone in his spotlight after the 40 seconds is up, they have to come and sit in the prison.

☆ To free prisoners, a Rescuer reaches the prison without being spotted.

☆ If the Guard catches everyone, pick another Guard and the game starts all over again.

If you are playing in an area where there is not much cover, you can give the Guard a smaller/weaker torch. This makes it more difficult to spot the Rescuers!

G.

Make sure you duck down low when the torch beam comes towards you. By the way, this is the same game as 40:40 on page 4 and Stealth on page 62, but played in the dark!

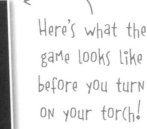

Here's what the game looks like before you turn on your torch!

FACT

• Dolphins sleep with one eye open. Never sneak up on a dolphin!

SCARPER

 **5-20**

> You are being led to prison by the enemy. Suddenly the Guard's attention is taken for 20 seconds, in which time you have to escape!

 ## WHAT?

☆ Lots of trees.

☆ All players camouflaged with as many leaves and branches as possible.

HERE'S AN IDEA:

As prisoners get better at dispersing into the undergrowth, the guard can count up to 10 to make it harder.

But if the guard wants to make it easier, because there is not much cover in an area, he could count to a higher number like 30 or 7,928.

HOW?

☆ Choose a player to be the Guard.

☆ The rest of the players must walk behind the Guard in single file through the trees, holding each other's shoulders.

☆ At any point the Guard can shout, 'SCARPER'. Then he must count to 20 as quickly as possible – he cannot turn around until he has finished counting.

☆ While the Guard is counting, the prisoners have to hide – behind trees, in bushes or in the undergrowth.

☆ When the Guard turns around he must search from where he is standing, and not move his feet. Those who manage to be invisible from the Guard are the winners.

DO NOT TURN OVER THIS PAGE

$$111,111,111 \times 111,111,111 = 12,345,678,987,654,321$$

MESSING WITH YOUR MIND

ONE:
Spin your foot clockwise and draw the number 6 with your finger in the air. What happens? Your foot should start spinning the other way all by itself. However hard you try to keep it going clockwise you won't be able to . . .

TWO:
Put an empty loo roll up to your right eye. Look at the far wall with both eyes open. With your left hand palm facing towards you, slide the hand to the middle of the tube. Can you see through your own hand?

THREE:
Get 3 bowls, put hot water in the first (not too hot for your hands), warm in the second and cold in the third. Start by putting one hand in the hot bowl and the other hand in the cold one. After a minute put both hands together in the warm bowl. One hand will think the water is cold and the other hot . . . mmmm . . . interesting!

HAD ENOUGH OF MESSING WITH YOUR OWN MIND?

Now it is time to start messing with other people's minds!

ELEPHANT MIND-READING
(You might need a calculator if you aren't very good at maths)

Like Geoffrey . . . ~~Sharky~~!

This is what you need to say . . .

1. Think of a number from 1 to 10
2. Take the number and multiply it by 9
3. Take the result and add the number together (i.e. 72 = 7+2, 9 = 0+9)
4. Take that number and take away 5
5. Take that answer and match it to the corresponding letter of the alphabet (1=A, 2=B, 3=C, 4=D)
6. Think of a country beginning with that letter.
7. Think of an animal that begins with the second letter of the country's name
8. Ask: 'Are you thinking about an elephant in Denmark?'

KEEP IT SECRET, KEEP IT SAFE.

This chapter is all about tricking your friends, winning sweeties and general skulduggery! We had to pretend the chapter didn't exist, so that if a friend or parent picked it up they would never find it! Do you think we fooled anybody?

This chapter does not exist. Nothing to see here!

THE SUPER NO ONE (SHHH! SECRET CHAPTER)

BALLOON SKEWER STICK

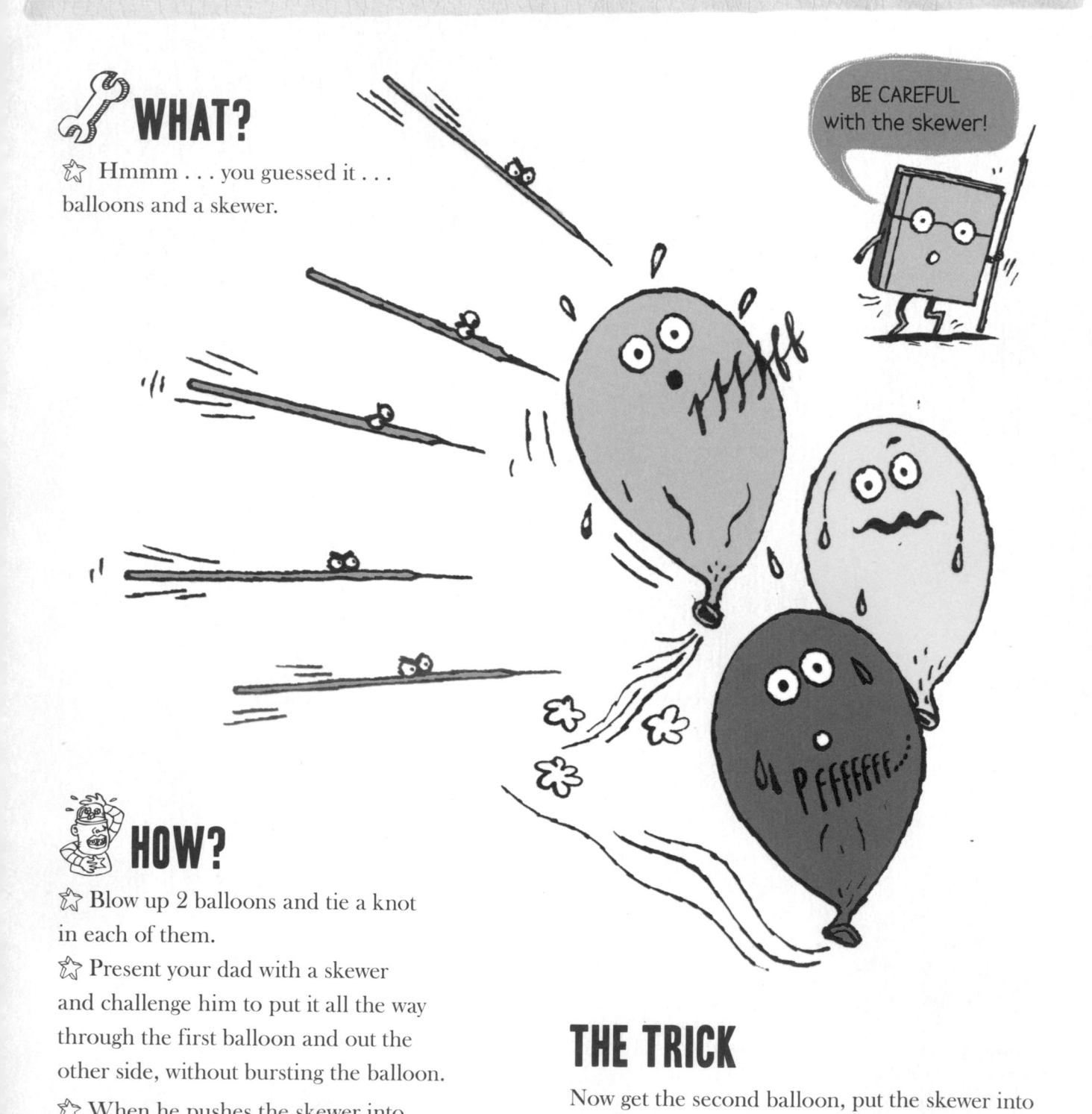

WHAT?

☆ Hmmm . . . you guessed it . . . balloons and a skewer.

BE CAREFUL with the skewer!

HOW?

☆ Blow up 2 balloons and tie a knot in each of them.

☆ Present your dad with a skewer and challenge him to put it all the way through the first balloon and out the other side, without bursting the balloon.

☆ When he pushes the skewer into the balloon, it will go POP!

THE TRICK

Now get the second balloon, put the skewer into it just next to the knot and push it out at the top. With a bit of luck it won't pop.

SPOON, FORK AND MATCH

I BET YOU A PACKET OF SWEETS . . .

If your stash of sweets is running low, this is an excellent way to win some from your parents or friends. Challenge them to see if they can do this trick or the one on the next page. If they succeed they get a packet of sweets, if they don't you win a packet of sweets.

THE CHALLENGE

You have to balance a spoon, a fork and a match on the edge of a mug/glass at ONE point . . . (don't use your parents' smartest glasses as there will be trouble if you break them!)

A FEW RULES

Nothing can touch the table except the mug/glass. The finished result must be free-balancing without any touching.

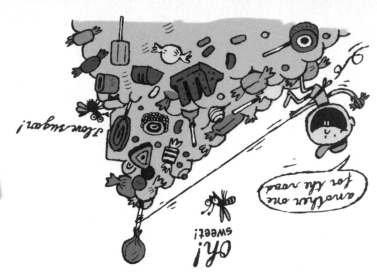

oh! sweet!

another one for the road

How sweet!

HERE IS THE SECRET . . .

Entwine the spoon with the fork prongs like this . . .

Place the match inbetween the prongs like this . . .

Balance them on the edge of the mug carefully!

SECRET CODE

 **WHAT?**

This is a brilliant and simple code. A page with holes is put over another page to reveal certain letters.

☆ A pen or a pencil with a sharp tip.

☆ This book!

 **HOW?**

☆ Can you see all the grey X marks on the next page (page 70)? This page is your 'code paper'.

☆ Using the pen or pencil, very carefully skewer through each of the grey X marks to create small holes.

☆ Place your 'code paper' back over page 72 and write down the letters that appear in the holes.

Hey presto! You have the answer to the riddle at the bottom of this page!

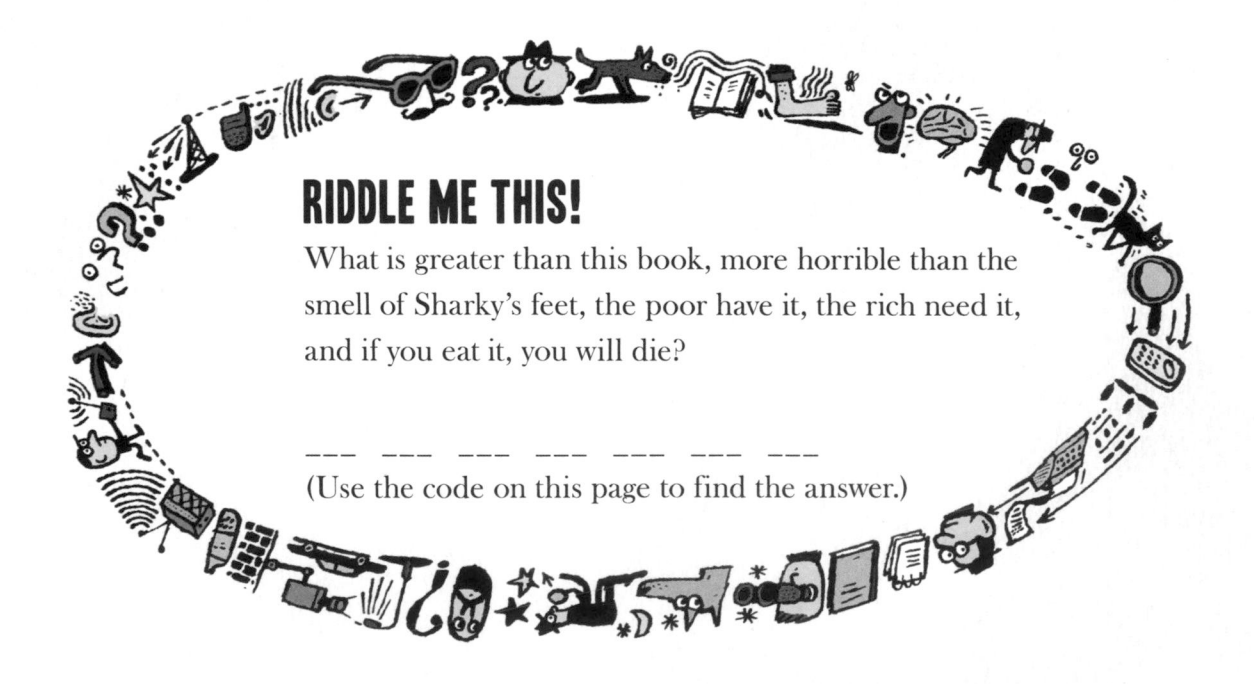

RIDDLE ME THIS!

What is greater than this book, more horrible than the smell of Sharky's feet, the poor have it, the rich need it, and if you eat it, you will die?

___ ___ ___ ___ ___ ___ ___

(Use the code on this page to find the answer.)

Great British Battles

The Battle of Waterloo was fought on Sunday 18 June 1815 near Waterloo in present-day Belgium, then part of the United Kingdom of the Netherlands. Don't worry, this book hasn't actually turned into a history text book, these two pages are here to turn to if a parent or teacher is coming close and you need to pretend you are doing homework! You can stop reading now, just pretend and wait until the grown-ups have gone and then you can get back to the good stuff. An Imperial French army

Look at the lovely horses, aren't they pretty. I like the grey ones best.

under the command of Emperor Napoleon was defeated by the Seventh Coalition, an Anglo-allied army under the command of the Duke of Wellington combined with a Prussian army under the command of Gebhard von Blücher. It was the culminating battle of the Waterloo Campaign and Napoleon's last. The defeat at Waterloo put an end to Napoleon's rule as

Emperor of the French and marked the end of his Hundred Days' return from exile.

Upon Napoleon's return to power in 1815, many states that had opposed him formed the Seventh Coalition and began to mobilise armies. Two large forces under Wellington and von Blücher assembled close to the north-eastern border of France. Napoleon chose to attack in the hope of destroying them before they could join in a coordinated invasion of France with other members of the Coalition. The decisive engagement of this three-day Waterloo Campaign (16–19 June 1815) occurred at the Battle of Waterloo. According to Wellington, the battle was "a game of two halves, really. It could have gone either way, but in the end the best side won".

On 13 March 1815, Napoleon was declared an outlaw. Four days later, the United Kingdom, Russia, Austria, Prussia and the Sheriff of Nottingham mobilised armies to defeat Napoleon. Napoleon knew that once his attempts at dissuading one or more of the Seventh Coalition allies from invading France had failed, his only chance of remaining in power was to attack before the Coalition mobilised. If he could destroy the existing Coalition forces south of Brussels before they were reinforced, he might be able to drive the British back to the sea and knock the Prussians out of the war. An additional consideration was that there were many French-speaking sympathisers in Belgium

Duke of Wellington, 1769-1852.
He is missing a bit of colour, moustache and sunglasses
. . . do your worst!

Napoleon delayed giving battle until noon on 18 June to allow the ground to dry, and Chelsea were playing Man U in the FA Cup Final before lunch. Wellington's army, positioned across the Brussels road on the Mont-Saint-Jean escarpment, withstood repeated attacks by the French, until, in the evening, the Prussians arrived in force and broke through Napoleon's right flank. At that moment, Wellington's Anglo-allied army counter-attacked and drove the French army in disorder from the field. Pursuing Coalition forces entered France and restored Louis XVIII to the French Throne. Napoleon abdicated, surrendered to the British, and was exiled to Saint Helena, where he died in 1821.

The battlefield is in present-day Belgium, about eight miles (12 km) south-east of Brussels, and about a mile (1.6 km) from the town of Waterloo. The site of the battlefield is today dominated by a large monument, the LION MOUND. As this mound used earth from the battlefield itself, the original topography of the part of the battlefield around the mound has not been preserved.*

*Thanks to Wikipedia for (most of) this information.

and a French victory might trigger a friendly revolution there.

Wellington intended to stop Napoleon picking up the Coalition armies by moving through Mons to the south-west of Brussels. This would have cut Wellington's communications with his base at Ostend, but would have pushed his army closer to Blücher's. Napoleon played on Wellington's supply chain concerns by giving him false intelligence. He divided his army into a left wing commanded by Marshal Ney, a right wing commanded by Marshal Grouchy, and a reserve, which he commanded personally (although all three elements remained close enough to support one another). The frontier was crossed near Charleroi before dawn on 15 June.

This photo is pretty inconclusive to be honest. The man wearing red seems to be in charge, though.

DOT CRICKET

It is just like REAL cricket! Without the stadium, the fancy dress and the commentators of course.

This is a way for cricket fans to put off doing their homework. It's also a great game for when you are a bit bored in class.

Ⓢ

WHAT?

6	C	1	
LB	4	3	W
2		LBW	2
B	1	4	B

☆ A grid similar to the one above. You can either use this or fill in the grid on the next page, if you want to move the boxes around.

W = Wide (1 run)   LB = Leg Bye (1 run)
B = Bowled (out)   C = Caught (out)
LBW = Leg Before Wicket (out)

☆ A pencil.   ☆ Paper.

HOW?

☆ First up, you need to choose your team and an opposition. 10 players in each team. In your team you can have all your friends and favourite players. Then pick a foreign team like Australia to play against.

☆ Write down the batting order for your team. It can be any order you like.

☆ To bowl, take a pencil and hover it over the grid. Then close your eyes, do a few circles in the air and strike! Whichever box the pencil lands in is your batsman's score. If you score a dot ball (blank square), 2, 4 or 6 runs, it is the same batsman's turn again. If you score a single run or 3 runs then it's the next batsman's turn. Make a list of the scores like this:

ME	1 1 1 . . . 4 6 2 B
Kevin Pietersen	1 3 2 . 4 4
Milo	6 4 C
Andrew Strauss	3 1 1 1 . 4 6 6 6 1 1 3

☆ If you hit **LBW, C**aught or **B**owled, then the batsman is out and the next batsman on the list is in. Once all 10 batsmen are out, write down a batting order for the opposition team down and get going again . . . DON'T BE BIASED, you have to give them a fair chance too.

73

Here is a grid for you to fill in yourself.

EXTRAS
If you are playing with a friend, flip a coin to see who bats first. If you are batting first, then they start with the pencil, close their eyes and 'bowl' into the grid. You then keep score for your team. Switch over when all of your team is out.

FACT

• You blink once every 6 seconds on average. This means that you will blink about 250 million times in your lifetime! I bet you blinked just then, hee hee.

brilliant batting

tshh

POC

zzzzzzzz

Don't get caught playing this in class! If you do, quickly turn back a page . . . your teacher will think you are doing some extra work with a bit of luck.

G.

FOLDING FRENZY

Only joking, it is actually impossible to fold a piece of paper more than 7 times . . . see if you can do more, and try with other flat things.

RECORD NUMBER OF FOLDS

Kitchen foil: .... Puff pastry: ....

Your pillow: .... Pancake: ....

A leaf: .... A flat fish: ....

A tyre: ....

I am not for folding

Make sure it's a FLAT one!

Make sure it's a dead one. NEVER fold a living creature, they really don't like it.

careful children folding is an art.

SHAPES FROM DOTS

 **WHAT?**

☆ A piece of paper.

☆ A pen.

 **HOW?**

☆ Join the blue dots by holding a pencil in your non-writing hand.

☆ Have a go at the red dots with your foot.

☆ Now attempt the green dots with the pencil in your normal hand.

Make your own dot 2 dot – join up the random dots on this page to make a shape. Use different colours to see if you can draw a scary monster.

I LOVE d☻ts and SP☻TS

Keep it as neat as you can!

G.

BOXES

HOW?

☆ Make a grid in your exercise book or just carry on with the one we've started. Take it in turns to join up 2 dots with a pen.

☆ If you complete a square, then put the first letter of your name in the box. If you complete a square then you get another go.

☆ Never add a third side to a box unless you have to, because the other person will finish it!

☆ Keep playing until all the boxes have letters. The person with the most boxes at the end wins the game.

☆ No diagonal lines allowed.

WHAT?

☆ Exercise book or paper.

☆ 2 different coloured pens.

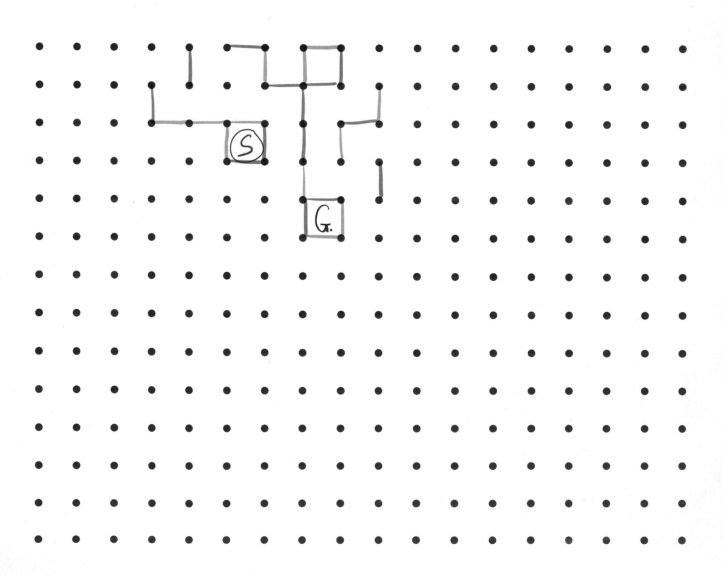

WATCH 'IT'

If you are wearing a watch and happen to be sitting in a sunny bit of the classroom, then you can reflect the sunlight. Dance it around on your teacher's back when they are writing on the board. Make sure you stop as soon as they turn around.

If someone else is reflecting their watch on the teacher's back, you can play 'It'. Try and catch the other person's reflection with your own.

AMBIGRAMS

Notice anything strange about the words below?

happy Birthday   *Sharky & George*

They read the same the right way up as they do upside down. Crazy! Try your own ambigram here.

TABLE RUGBY

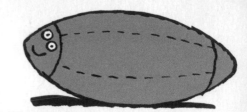

2

🔧 WHAT?

☆ A smooth table.

☆ A 2p or 10p coin.

A rugby game that is unlikely to cause any major injuries . . . This is a non-contact sport!

1 **2** **3** **4**

CLASSROOM GOLF

☆ Decide on a starting point – this is the tee. A desk works pretty well.

☆ Each person scrumples up a bit of paper into a ball and covers it in sticky tape to make it as smooth and round as possible.

☆ Use a ruler as your club.

☆ Invent holes and bunkers around the classroom. For example, another table, the teacher's desk or an upturned book.

☆ Land your homemade golf ball in the chosen hole with the fewest shots, avoiding any bunkers!

HOW?

☆ Take it in turns to place the coin just overhanging the edge of the table. To start the game, you have 3 chances to tap the coin across the table to the far side. Use the palm of your hand for the first shot, then your fingernails for the second 2 shots.

☆ To score a try you have to get the coin to overhang the far side of the table. Then you have to flick it into the air and catch it in the same hand. This scores 5 points.

☆ Spin the coin on the table and, while it's spinning, trap it cleanly between your thumbs.

To convert the try, the defending player sitting at the other side of the table makes a set of rugby posts with their arms and thumbs. The scoring player flicks their thumbs upwards to get the coin to fly through the 'posts'. This scores another 2 points.

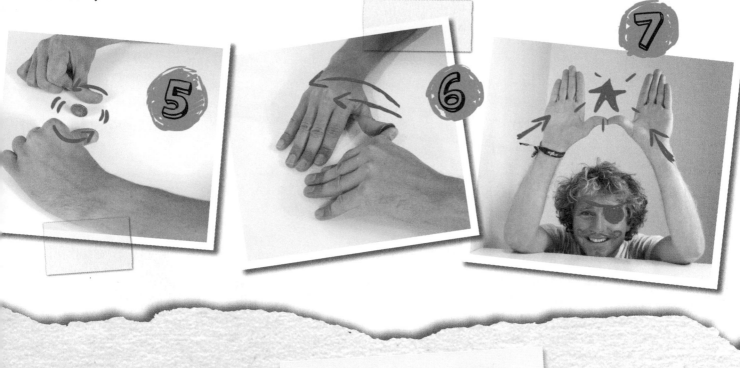

Get in the spirit of golf fashion by rolling up your trousers and pulling up your socks.

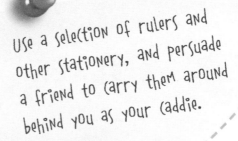

Use a selection of rulers and other stationery, and persuade a friend to carry them around behind you as your caddie.

TABLE FOOTBALL

 2

 **WHAT?**

☆ A smooth table.

☆ 3 coins, 2p or 10p.

> There is money in this game but definitely not as much as in the real thing.

 **HOW?**

☆ Have a look at the diagram below. You have two coins (a and b) that you push off from one side of the table with the palm of your hand, one at a time. Wherever they stop forms the first 'goal'.

☆ Take the third coin (c), and push it from the same table edge to get it through the goal. Keep trying with your fingernails to flick it through (a) and (b) until you score a goal.

☆ Make (a) the ball and flick it through the new goal, which will be between (b) and (c).

☆ Continue this until you reach the end of the table. Then let your opponent have a go. The person with the most goals over the length of the table wins.

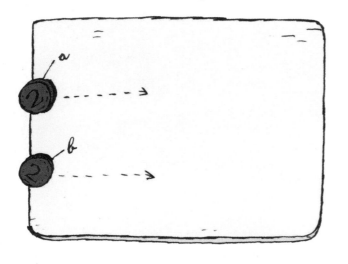

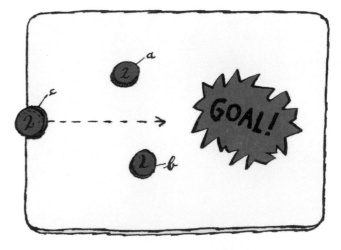

PRANK!

Get a pencil and 2 coins. Colour in the edge of one of the coins with the pencil. Then ask your victim to pinch the flat sides of the coin and roll it all the way from their forehead to their neck. You can demonstrate with the clean coin and then hand over the dirty coin. When they are finished they should have a pencil mark all the way down their face. Hee hee hee hee!

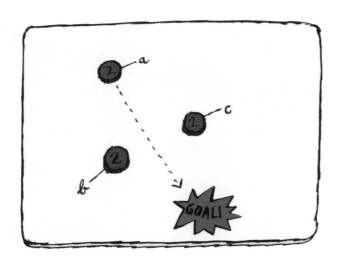

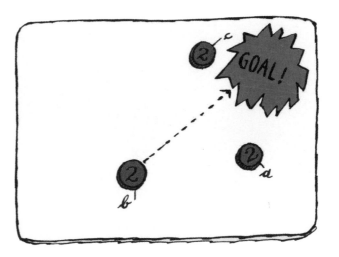

COIN RUBBINGS

Place different sized coins underneath this page. With the edge of a pencil, gently scribble over the top of the coins and it should create an outline.

See if you can find other interesting things for rubbing, for example:

* A metal watch-strap (from your mum or dad)
* A key
* A medal (if you've won one!)
* Some wood
* The sole of your shoe
* A jelly (or maybe a pet)

Take a biro or ballpoint pen and write on a banana skin. It feels really nice! Nature's notepad . . .

FACT

• If you stroke a cat 70 million times you will create enough static electricity to light a bulb for an hour.

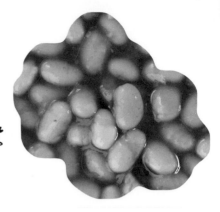

SHARKY & GEORGE

SHARKY & GEORGE

SHARKY & GEORGE